THIS CANDLEWICK BOOK BELONGS TO:

_____

_____

_____

_____

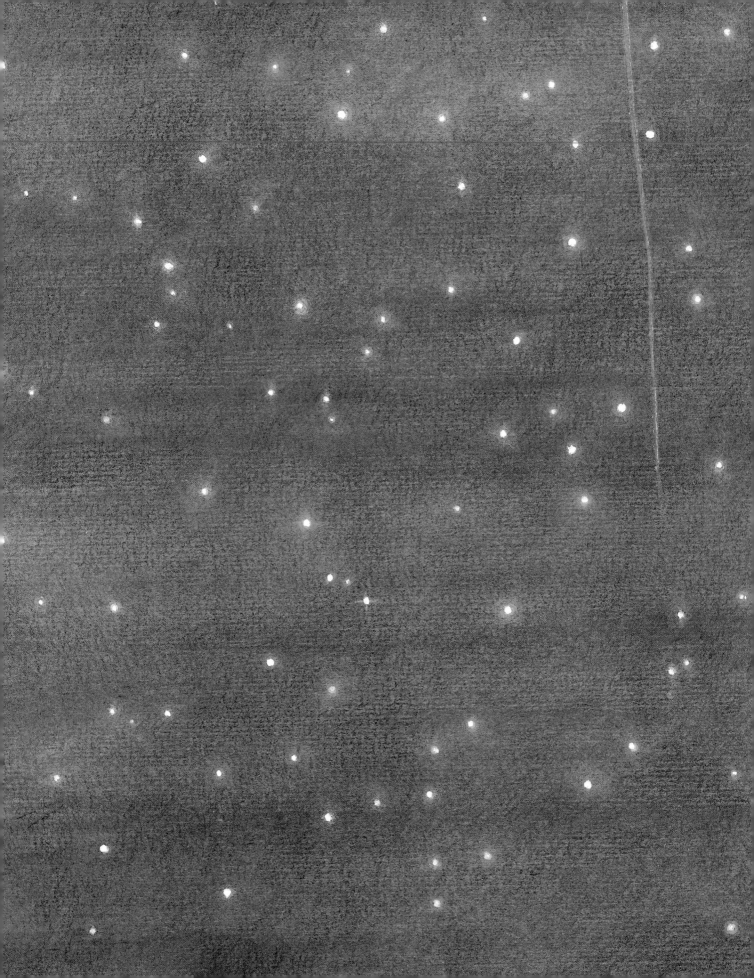

For
RALPH
and the
NATURAL
THEATRE CO.

First U.S. paperback edition 1996

The Library of Congress has cataloged the hardcover edition as follows:

Dale, Penny.
Ten out of bed / Penny Dale. — 1st U.S. ed.
Summary: A young child and nine stuffed animals fall asleep,
one by one, after playing a series of games.
ISBN 1-56402-322-2 (hardcover)
[1. Counting.   2. Bedtime—Fiction.   3. Sleep—Fiction.
4. Toys—Fiction.   5. Animals—Fiction.]   I. Title.   II. Title: 10 out of bed.
PZ7.D1525Te   1994
[E]—dc20   92-46116
ISBN 1-56402-834-8 (paperback)

2 4 6 8 10 9 7 5 3

Printed in Hong Kong

This book was typeset in Bookman Light.
The pictures were done in colored pencil and watercolor.

Candlewick Press
2067 Massachusetts Avenue
Cambridge, Massachusetts 02140

TEN OUT OF BED

Penny Dale

CANDLEWICK PRESS
CAMBRIDGE, MASSACHUSETTS

There were ten out of bed . . .

and the little one said, "Let's play!"

And Hedgehog said,
"Let's play TRAINS!"

So they all played trains
until Hedgehog fell asleep.

There were nine out of bed
and the little one said,
"Let's play!"

And Ted said,
"Let's play BEACHES!"

So nine played beaches
until Ted fell asleep.

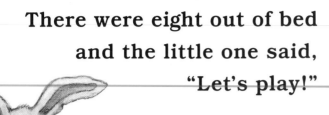

There were eight out of bed
and the little one said,
"Let's play!"

And Rabbit said,
"Let's play ACTING!"

So eight played acting
until Rabbit fell asleep.

There were seven out of bed
and the little one said,
"Let's play!"

And Bear said,
"Let's play PIRATES!"

So seven played pirates
until Bear fell asleep.

There were six out of bed
and the little one said,
"Let's play!"

And Sheep said,
"Let's play DANCING!"

So six played dancing
until Sheep fell asleep.

There were five out of bed
and the little one said,
"Let's play!"

And Croc said,
"Let's play GHOSTS!"

So five played ghosts
until Croc fell asleep.

There were four out of bed
and the little one said,
"Let's play!"

And Nellie said,
"Let's play FLYING!"

So four played flying
until Nellie fell asleep.

There were three out of bed
and the little one said,
"Let's play!"

And Zebra said,
"Let's play CAMPING!"

So three played camping
until Zebra fell asleep.

There were two out of bed
and the little one said,
"Let's play!"

And Mouse said,
"Let's play MONSTERS!"

So two played monsters
until Mouse fell asleep.

There was one out of bed and the little one said,

"I'm sleepy now!"

So he slipped under the covers next to Ted.

Good night, sweet dreams, ten in the bed.

PENNY DALE says her aim in this book was to show these less-than-sleepy animals playing and using their imaginations just as children would. "The small vignette in the corner of each spread represents reality; the rest of the page shows the much larger, more wonderful imaginary world." The creator of *Daisy Rabbit's Tree House*, *All About Alice*, and *Wake Up, Mr. B.!*, she is also the illustrator of *Once There Were Giants* by Martin Waddell and *The Mushroom Hunt* by Simon Frazer.